78460

DATE DUE

A Note to Parents

Read to your child...

★ Reading aloud is one of the best ways to develop your child's love of reading. Older readers still love to hear stories.

★ Laughter is contagious. Read with feeling. Show your child that reading is fun.

★ Take time to answer questions your child may have about the story. Linger over pages that interest your child.

...and your child will read to you.

★ Do not correct every word your child misreads. Say, "Does that make sense? Let's try it again."

★ Praise your child as he progresses. Your encouraging words will build his confidence.

You can help your Level 2 reader.

★ Keep the reading experience interactive. Read part of a sentence, then ask your child to add the missing word.

★ Read the first part of a story, then ask your child, "What's going to happen next?"

★ Give clues to new words. Say, "This word begins with *b* and ends in *ake*, like *rake, take, lake.*"

★ Ask your child to retell the story using her own words.

★ Use the five Ws: WHO is the story about? WHAT happens? WHERE and WHEN does the story take place? WHY does it turn out the way it does?

Most of all, enjoy your reading time together!

Fisher-Price and related trademarks and copyrights are used under
license from Fisher-Price, Inc., a subsidiary of Mattel, Inc.,
East Aurora, NY 14052 U.S.A.
©2003 Mattel, Inc.
All Rights Reserved. **MADE IN CHINA.**
Published by Reader's Digest Children's Books
Reader's Digest Road, Pleasantville, NY U.S.A. 10570-7000
Copyright © 2004 Reader's Digest Children's Publishing, Inc.
All rights reserved. Reader's Digest Children's Books is a trademark
and Reader's Digest and All-Star Readers are registered trademarks of
The Reader's Digest Association, Inc.
Conforms to ASTM F963 and EN 71
10 9 8 7 6 5 4 3 2 1

Library of Congress Cataloging-in-Publication Data

Hamilton, Tisha.
   Brian's big break / by Tisha Hamilton ; illustrated by Julie Durrell.
      p. cm. — (All-star readers. Level 2)
   Summary: After Brian injures his wrist playing baseball, he is worried that he will be
unable to be a great sports star.
   ISBN 0-7944-0375-1
   [1. Sports injuries—Fiction. 2. Accidents—Fiction.] I. Durrell, Julie, ill. II. Title.
   III. Series.

PZ7.H182659Br 2004
[E]—dc21

2003046802

Brian's Big Break

by Tisha Hamilton
illustrated by Julie Durell

All-Star Readers®

Reader's Digest Children's Books™
Pleasantville, New York • Montréal, Québec

Brian loved sports. He fell asleep thinking about sports. He woke up thinking about sports.

Brian played basketball.

He played baseball.

He played soccer.

Sometimes people asked Brian what he wanted to be when he grew up.

Sometimes he said a basketball star.
Sometimes he said a baseball star.
Sometimes he said a soccer star.

Brian's friends liked sports, too.
One day, they were playing
baseball in the park. Brian's friend
Tim was pitching.

Tim threw a pitch. Brian swung his bat. Smack! The ball sailed into the air.

It flew over Tim's head. It flew over Kelly's head. It flew over Jeff's head. It flew over the fence!

It was a home run! Brian's friends jumped and cheered.

Then they frowned. Their ball
was lost!

"I'll get it," said Brian.

He climbed over the fence and
found the ball.

It was hard to climb with a ball in one hand. But Brian would not let go.

At the top of the fence, Brian tried to hold on. But the ball got in the way and he fell.

"Ow!" Brian yelled.
The ball was safe! But Brian's wris
was hurt. By the time Brian got
home his wrist hurt a lot.

Brian's mother frowned.
"We better go to the hospital," his
mother said.

Brian and his mother went to the hospital.
"This wrist is broken," the doctor said.

"What?" Brian cried. "How can I be a baseball star with a broken wrist? How can I be a basketball star with a broken wrist?"

"Wear this cast for a few weeks," the doctor said. "When you come back, I'll tell you a story."

The cast wasn't that bad. Brian's teacher gave him extra time to finish his work.

His friends helped him, too.

Brian's friends all signed his cast.
"Get well soon!" wrote Tim.

Soon it was time to see the doctor again.
"This wrist is as good as new," she said.
"What about that story?" Brian said.

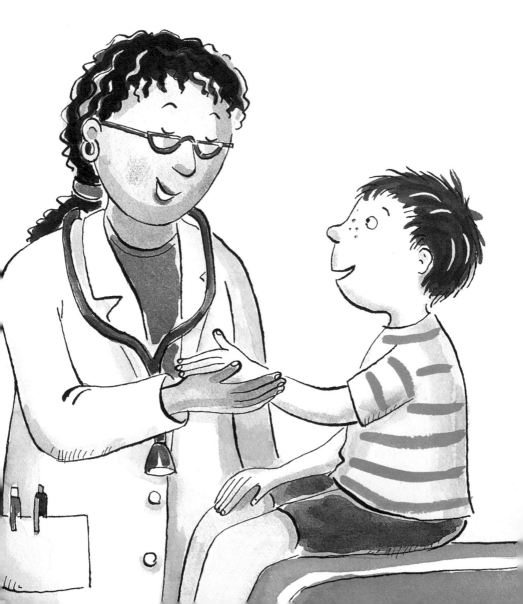

"When I was your age, I wanted to be a hockey player," she said.
"Then I broke my wrist."
"What happened?" Brian asked.

"My wrist got better," the doctor said. "I played hockey as well as ever."

"So how come you don't play hockey now?" Brian asked.

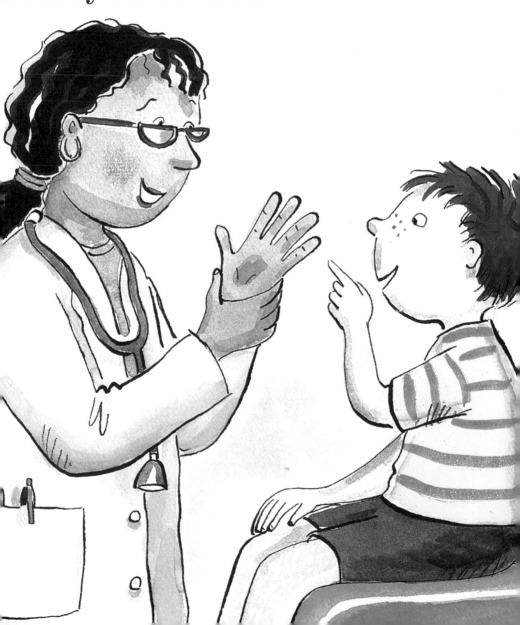

"I do!" she said. "I play twice a week for the Ice Crystals team. I'm their top scorer."

"Aren't you glad you can still be a baseball star?" Brian's mom asked. "Hmm," Brian said.

At home, Brian's dad asked,
"Aren't you glad you can still be a
basketball star?"
"Hmm," Brian said.

"Aren't you glad you can still be a
soccer star?" Brian's sister asked.

"Hmm," Brian answered.
"I think I'm going to be...

...a doctor!"

Words are fun!

Here are some simple activities you can do with a pencil, crayons, and a sheet of paper. You'll find the answers at the bottom of the page.

————— ★ —————

1. Circle the two words in each line that rhyme.

ball	call	bell
pitch	pail	itch
break	take	read
cast	cost	fast
glad	sad	said
fell	fall	spell

2. Find a word in the story that means the opposite of:

awake	smiled
lost	worse
fixed	sad

3. Draw a picture of yourself playing your favorite sport.

4. What happened next? Put the sentences below in the order things occurred in the story.

a. Brian hit a home run.

b. Brian broke his wrist.

c. Tim threw a pitch to Bria

d. Brian fell.

e. The doctor put a cast o
Brian's wrist.

5. Rearrange the words belov to make a sentence:

in	baseball	I
park	played	the